for
nilies
ıting
iation
adult
relationships ga...
that will help them manage...
conflict so their kids can continue with the
business of being kids.

Good-bye angry bugs

- By Andrea LaRochelle

ISBN: 978-1523763139

To my children, my greatest teachers – thank you for making me a better person – albeit somewhat crazy 90% of the time.

Sam is feeling angry. He has a grimace on his face, his body feels tense and he feels like a dark cloud is hovering over his head. The angry bugs have arrived.

Sam's mom said "Don't be angry, Sam. Just eat all the toast and leave the crusts." But the angry bugs stayed angry.

Sam's dad said "Chill out, crusts taste the same as the toast, they're just a different color." But the angry bugs wouldn't leave.

Sam's sister said "Relax, I didn't lose your spider-man toy." She offered to show Sam where his little brother had hid his toy. But the angry bugs stayed put.

Sam's grandma said "Being angry won't solve your problem. Wear your rain boots and I'll put your lucky shoes in the dryer, you can wear them tomorrow. " But the angry bugs continued to fume.

Sam's friend Cam said "There was nothing to be angry about, the sky was blue and the grass was green, perfect playing weather!" That made the angry smug, they weren't going anywhere.

Sam's neighbor Annie said "Sam, the angry bugs used to visit me too – I learned how to get rid of the angry bugs!" The angry bugs were still angry, but they were curious.

Annie told Sam she learned how to get rid of the angry bugs from her dog, Harry.

The angry bugs thought Annie was crazy, but they were listening.

Annie told Sam that her dog Harry would get angry each time someone walked in the alley behind their house. Harry would race to the back fence and pace back and forth with his tail between his back legs. Harry thought the alley belonged to him and didn't want any tresspassers.

Annie told Sam that she noticed whenever Harry saw or heard people in the alley and he got angry, he then growled – a deep, low growl. And after he growled for a bit, Harry wasn't angry any more. He'd stop pacing and start wagging his tail. The angry bugs started to panic. Annie was on to something.

Annie told Sam that once Harry the dog had a good GROWL to rid himself of the angry bugs, he was back to his happy self. The worry bugs hid their eyes.

Annie told Sam the angry bugs used to visit her a lot. The angry bugs would show up before bed when she didn't want to turn her lights out; when Annie's parents wouldn't let her have a play date; if she didn't get the library book she wanted at school; when Annie had to get up extra early in the morning. The worry bugs looked smug.

Annie told Sam that when she started to GROWL like Harry when the angry bugs would visit, the angry bugs would go away. The angry bugs were dreading Annie's next sentence.

Sam thought he'd try to GROWL, how hard could it be? He stood up and tried to GROWL, but ended up looking like a high pitched squeal. The angry bugs had a good laugh and stayed put.

Annie told Sam to pretend he was a fierce tiger and create a deep dark GROWL from the pit of his stomach. The angry bugs started to worry.

Annie told Sam to GROWL each time he felt the angry bugs coming to visit. Once, twice, 10 times, 100 times – as often as he needed to send the angry bugs away.

The angry bugs started to scramble.

Sam practiced his deep, dark stomach GROWL over and over. One last angry bug was hanging on for dear life.

Sam told Annie to listen to his deep, dark stomach GROWL that he had been mastering "Good-bye angry bugs." And the angry bugs were gone. Just like that.

Sam spent the next week perfecting his GROWL. He would GROWL as often as he remembered. And he would GROWL as soon as he felt an angry bug coming to visit.

And a really neat thing happened, Sam didn't get as angry much. Sam knew if the angry bugs did happen to show up in droves, he could GROWL them away and feel better. Good-bye angry bugs.

Made in the USA
Charleston, SC
30 November 2016